AADITYA GAJRA

As I Grew Up

An Anthology of Short Stories and Poems

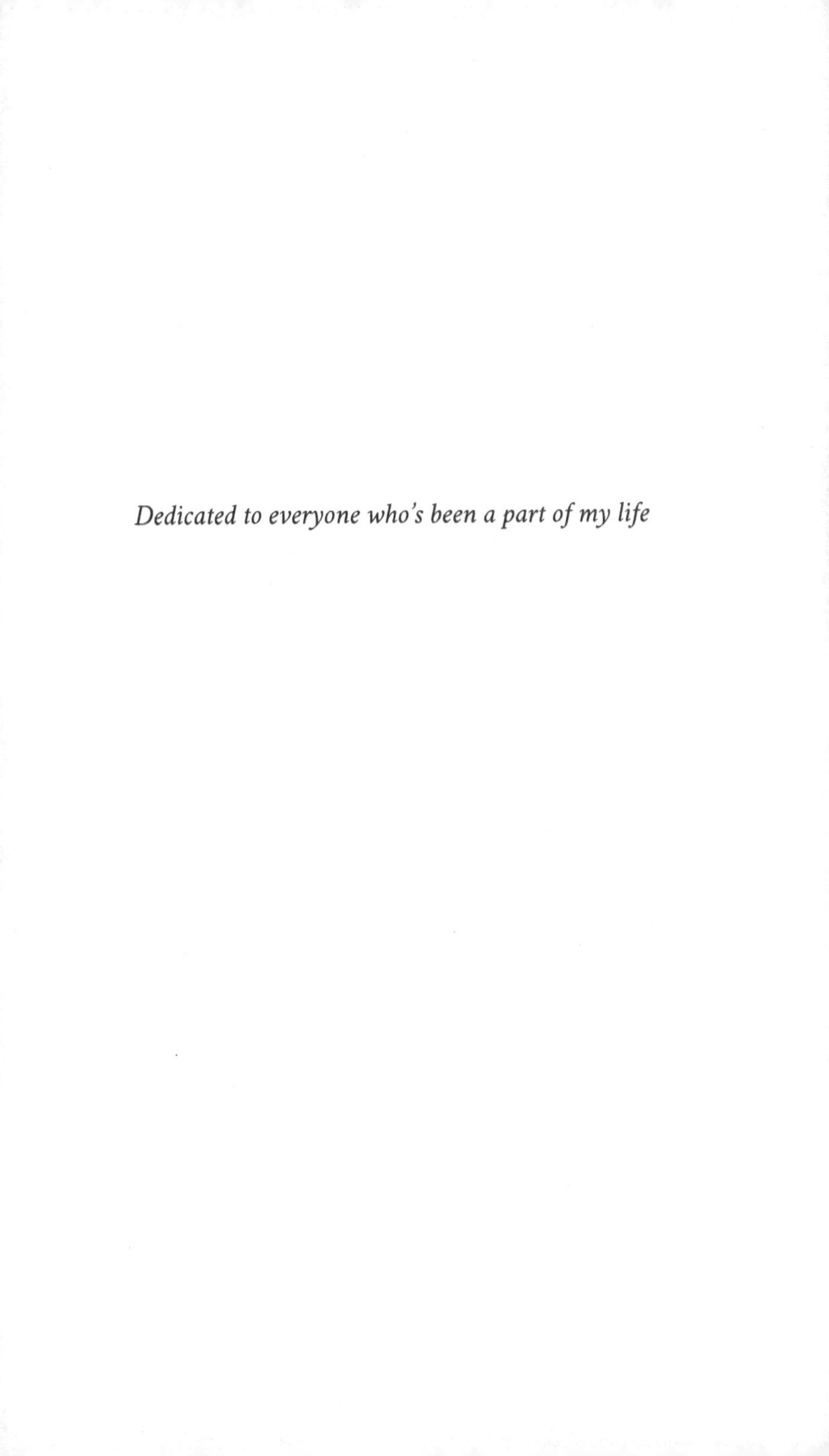

Dedicated to everyone who's been a part of my life

Contents

Foreword — iii
Preface — iv
Acknowledgement — v

1 I Can — 1
2 A Success Story — 6
3 Suspense: Albert Anastasia — 10
4 Mother Earth — 13
5 My Wish — 15
6 What a Mother is Like — 17
7 Lock-Not-So-Down — 20
8 What I Miss the Most About School — 22
9 Ticking Time — 24
10 Art — 26
11 Indian — 28
12 Neglect – A Pen's Autobiography — 30
13 Pulwama — 32
14 To Be You — 34
15 You — 35
16 Fata-Morgana? — 36
17 Rupees to Dollars — 38
18 Rainbow — 40
19 Tryst with Truth — 43
20 A Pome — 46
21 How Krishna Got His Name — 48

22 Holiday   50
23 Home Sweet Home   51
24 Sayonara   52
25 Topsy-Turvy   53
26 What I Feared when I was 10 and 15   54
27 Her Last Wish   55
28 Question   56
About the Author   57

Foreword

"As I Grew Up" is a compilation of short stories, poems and essay- by a very versatile young writer Aaditya Gajra. The anthology is designed for those who are on the journey of their personal discoveries, their evolution in terms of thought process, behavior, social awareness, their challenges, and their fears. This compilation is for an adult who has already gone through the journey and is able to relate to the writer as much as it is to a teenager who is going through the evolution process, to help them understand themselves and the situation better. It surely is a "must have" in your collection.

Best Wishes,

Srishti Jain

Preface

We all grow up. So do our thoughts. When I was a child, I always used to think that all cloud are cotton candies; one day I would climb up on them and eat to my heart's content. Then I would carry it with my bare hands and bring them down. Let mom taste these candies, she will forget Cadbury and Alpenliebe.

But as I grew up, I learnt that clouds aren't cotton candies. They aren't lightweight either. They are made up of gallons of water. And there my dream went kaput!

When I was a child, maybe 9 or 10 years old, I was accustomed to seeing boys and girls together. I never stopped to wonder why? As traces of adulthood began to show, seeing a boy and a girl together immediately sparked a flame in my mind. *Why are they both together? Planning something surely! Maybe they have become BF-GF.. hmm.. I must tell (name).*

This is precisely what I want to depict through this collection of stories, essays and poems. After reading the book, I'm sure you would realise how your thoughts have changed as well! Happy reading!

Acknowledgement

I would like to thank all those who made this anthology possible. First and foremost, thanks to my amazing family - Mom, Dad, Grandpa, Grandma and lil' brother of course! Secondly, I would like to thank all my teachers at school for guiding me on how to make my content better. Special thanks to Ms. Kavitha, Ms. Aruna and Ms. Pramila, Ms. Sarita and Ms. Sil Ramesh. A huge thanks goes to Mrs. Anjana, who has been a constant mentor since Grade 8. Special thanks to Ms. Srishti Jain, Founder/Director, Örva for all the love you've given and all that you've taught me. Thanks to Suchitra, Supraja, Benolin, Christina, Ashish and Karthik at Notionpress. Thanks to all those from whom I could learn and get inspired - Amish Tripathi, RJ Palacio, Kevin Missal, Pulkit Ahuja, John Green, Sudha Murty, Ruskin Bond, R.K Narayan, Rajani Thindiath, Benjamin Alire Sáenz and Jamila Gavin. I would like to specially mention Mr. MVS Murthy a.k.a Happymantata, who has been a guide throughout my literary journey. This book couldn't have been published without his blessings. I am lucky enough to have an awesome group of friends who have got my back at any point of time. I couldn't thank you enough. Gratitude to Vahini Bhaskerwar, who designed such an spectacular cover for the book. She's been a very spontaneous learner. My deepest thanks to Mother Nature, without whose permission I wouldn't have been able to complete this book and present it to you, my wonderful readers. A reader is the best gift an author could get. You are my gift. Thank you from the deepest recesses of my heart for picking this book up and reading.

1

I Can

The audience stood up in applause for me. I had never got this chance before, never. "Thank you everyone.", I bowed and exited the stage. "You did very well, Tom. I am proud of you.", Mrs. Smith said as I walked to my greenroom. I threw on my school uniform and headed to go to the ground, where mom was waiting for me. I wore a totally nervous look on my face. "I am so proud of you, honey! You were stupendous!", was the reply I got from Mom when I asked her whether I sang my song well or not. Mom was praising me all the while we got home. When we reached home, I straight went to my bedroom, threw on my pajamas, and fell on the bed. "Phew! What a tiring day", I thought as I went to take out my diary from the rack. I had promised mom that I would make an entry in the diary every day, and this was my first day. I took my pen and started writing away –

November 25th, 2009
Wednesday
When will you improve, Tom? I need to talk to your mother. Right

away! Dearest Tom, you have scored enough marks to humble Albert Einstein himself!

This was how all the teachers used to scold me in my school. I had never been a bright student, so this was all normal to me now. I was used to all this now. People making faces at me, my friends calling me a loser, teachers scolding me, my parents mocking me were some of the things that I didn't even care about now. I was always happy from outside, but something, probably my heart was not happy. I always lived in depression. I hardly ate anything. But, neither my parents and teachers, nor my friends noticed my dullness, ever. It seemed as if the whole world was against me. The golden moments in my life:

1. The times when I used to score 30 % in my exams.
2. When my little sister, Olivia was born.
3. Today, when I realized that "I Can"

The only period I liked in school was music, with Mrs. Smith. She never scolded me. What she did was only encourage me to move forward and forward. It was me who never paid any attention to her. Never mocking, nor scolding me. Only love, and love. She treated me as a special student. Sometimes, she used to call me to her house and tell me what I needed to improve, to do anything. These special behavior improving classes had great secrecy. Mom used to ask me about the things I used to do at Mrs. Smith's house. I never revealed that she behavioral classes for me. I used to make away with some lame excuse always, like I was playing the keyboard or stuff like that. I knew that Mrs. Smith was a blessing in disguise for me.

The special classes helped me a lot. The 10% I used to score in exams started to rise higher and higher, gradually. Even though it took me a lot of time, but I managed to lose the "Loser" title. Funny, isn't it? Losing the "Loser" title. Ha Ha!! Gradually, I started to raise my head in the school without fearing from anyone. My heart, too started to beat a little happily than it was before. I felt that a part of the world was now with me, and I now I wanted the whole world to be with me. I had shared this with mom once, and she was like, "The world is always with you. You just have to clear the obstacles that stand in the way." Yeah, maybe she was right. I just had to clear the obstacles that were standing and blocking my way to success.

And after a few months, I had done it. I had overcome my obstacles. I felt that the whole world was with me now. My confidence increased. I started to become a topper in class. My marks overflowed. The teachers were happy with me now. I no longer lived in depression. I mingled with everyone now. I owed Mrs. Smith big time. And that very day I noticed the change in myself, I ran to Mrs. Smith and said a huge thank you to her. "This is what teachers are here for. To improve children, to teach them values and ethics. I am happy that my classes brought a difference to your life, my dearest Tom." And that very day, Mrs. Smith called me and said, "Tom, I know the teachers have never given you a chance to perform on the stage. And that is why, I have chosen you to sing a song on the annual day of our school." This made me a bit tear-eyed. I thanked Mrs. Smith again and left the room.

There was no one except me in our class room. They all had gone to the dance class. I sat on my table and thought, "Why didn't I realize that 'I could' before this all stuff. There was no one to stop me. I myself was becoming an obstacle to myself. I was the judge. It was up to me, whether 'I could' or 'I couldn't'. The two paths, one of success and another of failure, were always open to me. I was the one who decided to continue on the path leading to failure. I am responsible for all this. Now, I see the consequences of walking on the path of failure. Failure was always shouting "Choose me" before me, but there was a little voice of success. I was the one who decided to ignore the voice of success." A sudden tap on my shoulder brought me back to the real world. I turned around to see who it was. It was Justin, my best friend. "Thinking about the past, buddy? ", he asked me. "No, I was making a list of songs to sing on the annual day of our school", I lied. " Nice try, Tom. You cannot hide the truth from your best friend. Tell me the truth", he caught me. The worst part of having people who truly understand you is that your privacy is hijacked.

"Yeah, I was thinking all about my past."

"The past can never be changed, Tom. What you can do is focus on the present to improve in the future.", and Justin went on. Finally, his lecture completed. The bell rang and it was time for us to return home. I waved bye to Justin till he was no bigger than a tiny speck of black on a white wall. All the time in the bus, I was thinking and noting down what came in my mind. I myself don't remember how many points I wrote. I was in a different world till someone, like woke me up from a trance and told me that my stop had arrived. After reaching home, I took out the diary in which I had written some points, and then made a recipe. I opened a fresh page of a fresh book in a fresh mood and wrote my secret recipe. The title - " How to accept yourself the way you are"

And then it had started. My first recipe was a big hit. I loved the recipe and teachers, the way I behaved. Guess what I did next? Well, I started to write more recipes. And also to mention, all of them were big hits. 101 hits, 0 flops. Then days came when I was given the "Most Disciplined Student of The Year" award, prizes for various competitions, and the most important – Praises from my teachers (except Ms. Smith. She praised me from the starting).

Love,

Tom

"Tom, have you gone to bed yet?" mom asked me from the kitchen. I replied, "No, momma dearest." "Go to bed now, Tommy." she said as I went to my bed.

Even though I wanted to sleep, I kept wondering of the moment when I and Mrs. Smith recited together, "I Can "

2

A Success Story

"A fresh morning. A fresh start", he thought as he walked along the footpath, watching the sun rise as the clouds floated in the blue sky. He heard the birds chirping and saw the cats and dogs waking up from their beauty sleep. He appreciated nature. He felt a new bundle full of energy within him. He felt, that today he would surely climb it. He had failed many times, but his sister did not let him lose hope. "The true meaning of success is not in not falling, but rising every time we fall." He kept on thinking about the summit, when a sweet voice interrupted – "Woke up early today, Ravi?" "Yeah, Rima", he replied. Rima was his sister. A cute, caring, affectionate and loving sister best described her. She was Ravi's mentor in life. He without his sister was like a fan without electricity, or a SIM card without balance in it. They were a team, and they worked together. Their goal was only one, that was to reach the summit. They wanted to climb and climb on together till they reached the summit of their minds, that is the summit within. They both took inspiration from Major HPS Ahluwalia, who was an Indian to reach the summit of The Great Mount Everest. In many of the Major's interviews, HPS Ahluwalia had described the difficulties faced when climbing a mountain. He had told that climbing the mountain within on our minds is as hard as climbing The Everest. By saying – "Reaching the summit within", the Major meant gaining control over the human mind and emotions. Ravi and Rima, both fascinated and inspired by Ahluwalia's words, decided to climb the summit within. Gaining control over emotions and the wishes of the mind is not very easy. It happens gradually, and never happens in the blink of a human eye. "Nothing is impossible.", Rima used to say to Ravi to encourage him. Ravi never gave up hope, only because of the self-control his sister and he had developed inside him. The brother-sister duo also loved reading books. Their love for reading books helped develop their self-confidence and self-esteem. Their passion of reading books helped them become intelligent. Their wish to read books gave them much General Knowledge. They loved books, and so did their parents. Ravi had read about Major HPS Ahluwalia when he was in class five, and since then, he had been keeping himself updated on the Major. He told about this to his sister, who was then in class eight. Since then, they both never stopped trying everyday to reach the summit within. Both their parents succumbed to the eternal sleep, but even then, the Sis–Bro didn't give up. Even almost 40 years later, Ravi and Rima, at the age of 70 and 73 respectively kept trying. They faced many difficulties in life, and they had to cross them. The barriers included financial, family, health and social problems. They crossed them and tried to clear all the barriers that stood in the way. Clearing all the obstacles was their priority, so that once all the barriers were clear, they would find themselves on the peak of the mind. As they both turned old, it became even more challenging to maintain a grip on the summit within. They worked hard, and never gave up on the commitment they had made to themselves - To maintain their grip on the hard mountain of the mind. They both had still not left their passion for reading books, but yes, their tastes of types of books had certainly changed. When they were young, they liked to read books which had fantasy, or animals in them. But as for now, they liked to read serious books, like the Study Book of Psychology, and The Difficulties of Life. Gone were those days, when they were busy in their regular routine. Wake up at 7 am, get ready and go to work. Work all day, sacrifice your time, and get the hard-earned money you deserve. Waking up at 7 in the morning meant going to bed early, which meant little or no Television, which in turn defined "No Entertainment". Their schedule was very hectic and they would get very tired after coming home. They would sit and write down all the expenses made in the day. At the end of every week they would go out for roaming about, and also sometimes for a movie, but provided they had saved at least *Aath Aana* (50 paise) in the week. 50 paise was considered as a great amount those days, and they were only spent if needed. Going to a movie, owning a car and watching the television were great luxuries those days. People often went to parks for outings. Kids were content with what they had. Video Games were yet to be invented, so children and even adults preferred playing outdoors. Everything was "Simple and *Saada*". No complications. No confusions. Only peace. No CD players or no DJs for music. Not many TVs and no mobiles for entertainment. They both would together earn 2.25 rupees per day, and hardly 7-8 paise was saved every day. The rest of the money would be spent for buying necessary items. The absence of their parents made them discouraged, but thinking about their role model brought them back on their track. They spent the day at leisure whenever there was a holiday from work. They always had some funds reserved for critically important situations. Some amount from the savings of each week was kept aside for the celebration of festivals. Ravi and Rima had something to talk about every time they got some peace. They not only thought about the present, but also about the future. They both became role models for people who wanted to live a peaceful life. In the process, they unknowingly reached the summit within. They unknowingly gained control over their emotions and feelings. They maintained a good grip over it. Never spoke more, never spoke less. 'Nothing wasted, nothing wanted' was the motto. They listened to each others' thoughts, and then took decisions. In case of social decisions, they took part in the discussion and freely expressed their opinion. They didn't get scared of speaking up in the public. They might have failed to cut the mustard many times, but they accepted their mistake and tried to improvise. They thought about the consequences of their each decision. They worked as a team. They never said "I". They always said "We". This very team spirit of theirs helped them to become successful in life.

3

Suspense: Albert Anastasia

I t was a graveyard, no wonder creepy sounds never stopped coming from there. Only three brave people had dared to go there. But after returning, those three were not as before. They had changed a lot. And the tales the three men told, sent shivers down everyone's spines. But, there was one tale that one of the three people told. And that tale made everyone's blood cold.

"It was 25th of October, 1960, the death anniversary of the famous mobster, Albert Anastasia. His body was buried in the Greenwood Cemetery, as we all know. Even after many years, his soul was still not free. It still haunted the cemetery. No one dared to even pass along the cemetery in the night. People believed that passing along the graveyard after 7PM would make the person's life haunted and horrible. Even after that, we three went to the graveyard to check it. It was very dark. The cold winds were roaming here and there, making our bodies cold. It took us fifteen minutes only to gather courage to go inside. Each of us had a torch to light our way. When we stepped inside the cemetery, our torches shut down which made us even more scared. We had charged the batteries before, but also the torches shut down! Each of us was thinking this to be a work of the ghost. But we went further to check the place. After walking for some time, we reached a place where the road forked into three paths. One went straight, the other went right and the another one went left. After much thinking, we decided to split our paths. I went straight, and my other two companions went left and right. As I continued on my path, I heard many sounds which gave me shivers. As I pushed my hand through the stuff in my bag to find my emergency flashlight, I realized that it was missing. I clearly remembered that I had put the flashlight inside. Again the thought of this being the work of a ghost came in my mind which made me even more scared. I thought of running here and there, and in the blink on an eye, bushes with spikes rose all around me and covered me from three sides. I started moving forward on the only way left open by the bushes, shivering. Each small sound was sucking the breath out of me. As it had been one hour since I started walking, I decided to take a nap and have some snacks. As soon as I lay on the grass, I fell asleep. But before sleeping, I remembered the name of the person near whose gravestone I was sleeping (just in case. It was a graveyard after all). It said – "Thomas May ". My short nap turned out to be nearly 2 hours, I guess. After the (long) nap, I was shocked when I woke up! Instead of Thomas May's gravestone, I was dumbstruck to find A. Smith's one due to which I fainted and fell down. When I regained consciousness, all my energy was drained out. Somehow, I managed to get out of the cemetery by taking breaks in between. It was hard, but finally I able to reach out. As I was proceeding to the village, I fell down on the road. Fortunately for me, some people from my village were passing from there in the noon and saw me. They immediately called for medical assistance and after a while, I was absolutely fine. I was very thankful to the villagers and thanked them again and again. But, the problem was not yet solved. My companions still had not come out of the cemetery. After seeing my condition on my return, no one was willing to go inside the cemetery. As there was no other option, we had to wait for them to return. After many days, my companions returned and now, the problem was solved and everyone was happy. No one has ever since dared to go inside the cemetery."

4

Mother Earth

Mother Earth, Mother Earth
You gave me birth
The dates of solstices and equinoxes are hard to remember
But, the dates can be remembered sitting near your peaceful rivers
You sacrificed everything you had
And learning everything about you made me mad

Mother Earth, Mother Earth
There is a lesson about you which I read, called – "Major Domains of The Earth"
And at that moment, knowledge about you in my mind took birth
Trees grow on plains
Which bring us rains
I realize that you have gone through much pain,
But, I'll never let your efforts go in vain

Mother Earth, Mother Earth
    You are so beautiful
    I know that we, humans are not being dutiful
    We throw garbage here and there,
    And when we are questioned, we say – "When and where?"

Mother Earth, Mother Earth
    I'll try my best to keep you alive,
    Because, you gave me a precious and priceless gem,
    Life

5

My Wish

Surviving in the harsh weather conditions,
　　You grow up
　　Through rains, droughts and floods
Initially, you are as small as a bean,
And eventually grow up to be a humongous tree
I applaud your growing up
A seed, a plant, and then a tree
If I'd be in your place,
Then I'd never be out of composure
You face humiliation
People call you a tiny seed and dispose you away,
But in the end,
It's you who gives them shade
You are a seed at the starting,
And grow up into a sapling,
You will gradually turn into a plant
The roots of your knowledge are going deeper and deeper,
As you suck the water of wisdom, from the soil of intelligence
You grow higher and higher to be a mighty tree,

You turn old,
And being called "Wise",
Because Old is Gold,
And you are one of them
If I had one wish,
I'd wish,
I want to be one of your kinds.

6

What a Mother is Like

The world is mine,
    I shall live in it as I will.
    Move as I will
Love it as I will.

The sky is mine,
    I shall fly as I will.
    Fly high as I will,
    Reach heights as I will.

The land is mine,
    I shall walk upon as I will.
    Break it down as I will,
    Burden it as I will.

Ye say all this nonchalantly,
    This is the land you walk upon.

The air you live upon,
The water you live upon.

Thou see the never coming,
    Or not; I am ignorant
    But I see the ensuing,
    And what I discern lies below.

The mother says -

"Ye all are mine,
    I shall rear thee as my own.
    Thou take care of thy mother,
    And I shall return it back.

Should ye lay waste me,
    The clock, shall tell,
    Ye, what a nurturer's wrath
    Feels like.

Crush thy mother, Quell thy mother
    Drive thy mother to coup de grâce.
    Shall ye do what ye state,
    Ye shall never be there to see the sequel.

Feed thy mother, Cherish thy mother
    Drive thy mother to an elated existence
    Shall ye do what ye state,
    Ye shall ever live blithe lives."

7

Lock-Not-So-Down

When you be someone who is beyond you, then you are someone you aren't. How good it feels to be someone you aren't! And when you expand your mindset and your limits, the nation prospers.

I want to communicate to you, through these lines, that one thing I realized during quarantine is that everything depends upon how you look at it. During this lockdown due to the major Corona crisis, some people may feel that productivity has shut down and almost all people have turned into zwodders. But, if we look at the other side of the coin, we may say that the world has completely and positively changed. People have changed. We are constantly acquiring new skills and achieving accomplishments. We are realizing the 'Power Within Us'. It is very pleasing to see how smaller the world has become by coming close to each other, that too by socially distancing one from the other. Families are much closer than they were before.

Let me take the change in my life as an example. No doubt, I have very much turned not lazy, but slow. On the other hand, now I proudly boast of all the skills of the household tasks that

I have. My daily routine has changed a lot. My daily tasks such as brushing, bathing and breakfast keep me occupied for quite a while. I seldom do yoga as well. I stay occupied for the rest of the day with tasks like mopping the house, cleaning the furniture, lunch, sleep, television and mobile phone. The most challenging part is from noon to 2PM and from 5PM to 8PM. 5 hours of free time! I possibly cannot be gadget – occupied all this time. And neither can I be study – occupied for 5 hours straight. And so, I have to think of innovative solutions to my boredom. My brain constantly works to think of ideas like art, craft and origami, making YouTube videos, helping my family members and spending time with my younger brother. I learnt many new indoor games, like carroms and cards. I also spent time in the kitchen and made many new dishes. Now, who says that productivity in lockdown is absent?

8

What I Miss the Most About School

"*The beautiful thing about learning is nobody can take it away from you.*"
     - B.B. King

The world evolves, and so do we! We live in the virtual world where Zoom, Meet and Webex are the latest sensations. People of all age groups, from children to elders have been hit bad. But children and online classes seem to be the gist of today.

Group activities and PET classes have become things of the past. We, as children, may or may not accept it, but we do miss school! As I reminisce about the past year of school, many memories come flooding to my mind. I miss the suffocating atmosphere of our tightly-packed class, and how cool a breeze seemed to be once we got out. I remember, all the teachers, looking at us with glaring eyes, as if ready to pounce upon us the next moment. And then there were excuses. Oh! We had a choice of excuses; all that could be said legit, of all topics under the sun. Messing with the person sitting next to us, laughing and giggling while the teacher droned on about her subject.

Then the library! The leader, shoving us all into the library, while we resisted. All sorts of books that I could devour. I even got a prize for the best reader of the year for reading 110 books in a year. Oh! And here at home, I get only a few books per month. After all, it's home, not school, where you could read books without actually purchasing them! The prizes are something that I miss the most! There was a boring assembly everyday, where I could see all the children scratching their heads like monkeys, getting bored. It was after I saw myself, that I came to realize that even I was doing the same! Then there were the worst, the tattletales. Oh, can't a person do what he wishes without a thousand cameras watching him all the time?

But again, as said by the great author Mark Twain, A man who carries a cat by the tail learns something he can learn in no other way. We all have to learn to bear with online classes, where the modem and router are two demons whom you have to fight with everyday to get through the gates of internet. It is no fun, I understand, but isn't learning something new better than learning nothing?

9

Ticking Time

No time to stand alone,
   Watch with our eyes
   The serene creation,
Has no longer value.

No time to look deep,
  Deep within your thoughts
  No time to share with her,
  The universal mother.

No time to look around,
  And admire the dance
  Of the beautiful green parents,
  When they bathe in the rain.

No time to reconnect,

With the friendly rocks.
Huge, huge rocks,
Are just a medium for fame.

No time to seek time,
    The most beautiful creation
    Much time to seek money,
    The most dangerous boon.

No time for the world,
    Except for midnight
    Hello, hi and bye,
    Then click and omit.

No time to satisfy our needs,
    Wants, wants and wants
    No time to live with peace,
    Without a gadget.

The clock's ticking,
    We don't have much time
    It's our chance,
    To save the paring creation.

10

Art

The time of 90s
    Moving hands, colourful canvas;
    Did not exist,
For none of the artists were born.

The black-white era,
   The rule of the English
   Cruel swords, inhuman hands,
   For this was the generation of darkness.

A beam of sunlight,
   The birth of,
   The colourful painters;
   The shaping canvas.

The wait for dawn,

Intolerable, inhumane
It was yet due,
The fight for colours.

The beginning of dawn,
    Struggles, yet marching
    Towards the freedom
    Of vivid imagination.

The wait for warmth
    A painter's struggle
    Uncountable protests,
    Infinite sacrifices.

Finally, dawn
    The rule of democracy
    The rule of citizen painters,
    Where everyone showed their colour.

11

Indian

One each, one all
  Let's bind out voices together;
  The song of our nation,
We sing with pride.

One each, one all
  Stand together,
  Salute to it
  The tricolour flag.

One each, one all
  Blend in
  The vivid tradition
  Of thy great mother.

One each, one all
  Admire, praise
  The bravery of our warriors,
  Day or night.

Let's see ourselves,
   Let's see our country
   This beautiful motherland,
   Is after all humane.
   One each, one all
   Let's bind out voices together;
   The song of our nation,
   We sing with pride.

One each, one all
   Stand together,
   Salute to it
   The tricolour flag.

One each, one all
   Blend in
   The vivid tradition
   Of thy great mother.

One each, one all
   Admire, praise
   The bravery of our warriors,
   Day or night.

Let's see ourselves,
   Let's see our country
   This beautiful motherland,
   Is after all humane.

12

Neglect – A Pen's Autobiography

I remember those old, rusty parchments of books. I remember the names of most refills that ever came to power my fountain nib. I remember all the suffocating, yet cozy days in my master's pouch. I remember the days of my youth. I was born to a poor family in a small hospital of about ½ an acre. I was one of the most dull-looking pens in the factory. Yet, I was thrown on to the harsh rollers that packed me into very crowded boxes which never contained anybody who talked to me. After hours of travelling, I finally reached a place, humans call "warehouse". I came to know that most of the pens I had come with had already been sold to retailers. We were again kept on the rollers that would group us according to our categories. As I rolled down, seeing the last lights of my life, I was suddenly picked up. I noticed a shady man who picked me up. I immediately came to know that he was stealing me. He quickly went to a silent room and took me out. "What a beauty! I'll keep it.", he exclaimed. From that day, I followed my master no matter where he went. He trusted only his diary and me to keep his secrets. I was the one who signed for him. Refills came and went, and so did pens in my master's life. His love for me decreased with time, and now as a worn-out pen, I lay in a corner of some damp drawer in the depths of my master's tiny house.

13

Pulwama

Disclaimer – This poem was written a day or two after the Pulwama attack occurred. The attack electrified the whole country. The poet expresses his anger towards the dastardly terrorists, but does not promote violence or killing of any sort, or shame any country/region.

This doesn't make any sense at all,
    Attacking an unarmed army
    And if you don't know basic manners,
    Pakistan, you're gone.

The almighty is watching you
    He helps everyone
    He will punish you
    By taking the form of Indian army.

Beware, beware Pakistan,
    Your bad time has come,

For the Indian Army
Has been given freedom to fight.

Airforce, navy, army
    Everything is ready
    You don't expect me to tell
    When it will surround you.

All the Indians are
    Raging with fire
    You have moved your soldier,
    We will move our queen.

All these years,
    You have defied us.
    With your pevish attacks,
    You have angered us.

Indians sure look diverse,
    But we all are one
    Beware, beware Pakistan
    For your time has come.

14

To Be You

Wouldn't it be so wonderful to be you,
   Fly in the skies of azure blue
   Wouldn't it be so wonderful to be you?

The gushing waterfalls and green fields,
   You soar past, whizzing by
   Open wings, blowing wings,
   Your exterior is the most beautiful dye.

Oh birdie! What wouldn't
   I give to be you,
   Oh birdie! What wouldn't
   I give to this land bid adieu.

Wouldn't it be so wonderful to be you,
   Fly in the skies of azure blue
   Oh, my dear birdie,
   Wouldn't it be so wonderful to be you?

15

You

The bright sun, gleaming eyes
   The demilune moon, crooked smile
   The roaring rivers, majestic hair
You, only you, nothing otherwise.

16

Fata-Morgana?

Though the chances are
    Less that it happens, let me tell you
    What if a train
Comes towards you?

The convoy is
    A couple quarter-miles away
    I learnt it in the 8th, it'll take
    A half-moment to reach ya. Once it
    Stands in front of you, investigate if
    It's a real one
    Sometimes, the occipital
    Might cause a phantasmagoria. Or maybe
    The convoy is real. Then it'll cause
    A gruesome scene,
    Not certainly can I delineate
    It.

Or instead, ye could

Sidestep, away from the parallels. Then
Watch the loco zoom
Into yer sight. After which,
Chronicle its bonafide for all
Its worth.

<h1 style="text-align:center">17</h1>

Rupees to Dollars

M-O-N-E-Y. Money.

Some say money cannot buy you everything. Some say money can buy you anything and everything. Why, justify? You just got hurt, you want the pain to go away. How? Simple! Get a doctor to come home (nothing some extra rupees cannot manage), get her/him to give you a nice sleeping injection. They call it mida-something. Yes, Midazolam! Sounds like a superhero name. Shazam! Midazolam!

You just lost something that had a lot of your memories attached to it. You are crying inconsolably. How do you get money to buy that back, ha? Simple! Get your memories erased by some so-called science technique developed by those American scientists in white lab-suits. Those lab suits are nothing but a piece of white cloth tied fashionably or buttoned atrociously. Why call them lab suits in the first place?

Next, if you're feeling terribly depressed or sad about anything, can money cheer you up? Not exactly. You can't fold a note and stick it on your face and publish that you are smiling!

However, money does buy you stuff that can make you happy.

Next case (most familiar with Indians) – Hunger with a capital H. Can money buy you freedom from hunger? Of course, you cannot satisfy your stomach by shoving down 100-rupee coins and 20000-rupee notes. Nonetheless, you can go to a 5-star (or with enough money, even a 9 or 10-star) restaurant and order such exotic dishes that you need an interpreter to eat them. Another option is to hire a personal chef and get the best dishes made for you.

I say, no – This all isn't if not impossible, then practical. You might have all the money in the world, I do not deny that. I do not care. But of what use is your money if there's nothing to buy? Suppose Midazolam injections haven't been invented yet. There are no medicines to make one sleep. Then what are you gonna do? Inject yourself with a fresh, crisp 500-rupee note with its edge? Gonna eat money if you're hungry? Gonna paste a strip of paper on your face to make it look as if you're smiling? That's insane. Are you going to get an appointment with someone from the deaths department and give him two briefcases filled with money, saying – Is this enough to wake him up from his eternal sleep? Money won't buy you someone's life. Maybe you can take someone's. But give back? Well....

Doesn't matter to me what people say. It shouldn't to you as well. All that matters is the happiness you have in your life. I admit, and am not looking down while saying this – Money is a factor. A very important one indeed. But is it so important that you leave everything behind, in hope that some pieces of paper will buy you everything you've lost by being far from them?

18

Rainbow

The leaves on the tree rustled quietly in response to the gentle breeze blowing outside. There was a deathly silence all around. Actually, what is a deathly silence? No idea. I could hear the fan rotating diligently, at a speed of 4. It caused the papers on the sofa to get lifted from their edges, a bit, but it wasn't enough to make them fly away. I was just sitting on the chair. No mobile to use, no TV to watch, no books to read, no person to talk to. Sometimes I wondered if this was what it felt like after death. Complete silence. *Sannataa*. No noises. I felt like eating something – Biscuits, no. Spicy and crunchy mixture, no. *Gud* and Groundnuts, no. Roasted paneer, yes. But there was no paneer in the house. After spending a couple minutes in the store-room, I gave up, thinking that when I would be truly hungry, I would eat. Not now. I came back to the hall and sat down.

I looked out of the open balcony door. The leaves weren't rustling anymore. There was no longer a gentle breeze, blowing across the lush greenery. I could no longer hear the swish-swish of the leaves. Instead, I heard the whoosh of loud winds. A storm was coming up. The wind was not gentle as a parent, but ferocious as a lioness whose children had been dared to attack upon. It no longer caressed the trees; it whacked them – whacked them till some of them slept forever to wake up as someone else.

And then it happened. The clouds turned black; yes, those very same clouds, which as a child I thought to be cotton candies, pink and white, suddenly turned ugly yet fascinating black. I felt a strange sense of excitement in me. I was 10, but never had experienced a storm. Everyone I knew kept bragging about how they had survived a storm, or an earthquake, or a tsunami, flood, drought and what not. Everyone tells you what they experienced; nobody tells you how to enjoy it. Because storms, tsunamis, floods, earthquakes and all these are Disasters, with a capital… or rather all capital letters. You don't get to enjoy disasters. Disasters only cause grief. When there's an earthquake, some unknown force places a ban on laughing, which if you break, invite unapproving glances from those who're sharing that experience with you.

Coming back to the storm, it was nowhere near what people had described. My aunt had told me, she once experienced a very, quote unquote, horrifyingly and astonishingly awful storm. Awful was the adjective she'd used. She'd said, it was one of the worst experiences of her life. It was gloomy all around and everyone was scared. There was no electricity in the house, she'd said. Now I see the point of complaining – There's no electricity. But why do people actually get affected by it? That's because they want to be in their artificial worlds, which is their comfort zone, where Alexa and Google Assistant and what-not are waiting like servants at your feet, ready to do your bidding. People can't stay away from their AI world for a while? I agree, even I used to think that way, until today, until now. I love the raw power of a storm. I've heard that monsoon is the season of rains, of storms. But I've also heard that it's the season of romance. What if people's wishes to make monsoon disappear came true? Those who long for monsoon would be utterly disappointed. It was pouring heavily. I stood there, perplexed, eagerly watching the trees dance in happiness, and bow their heads in mourning for their friends who had succumbed to the rain, waiting for the rainbow to appear. I was not disappointed.

19

Tryst with Truth

I often ponder over it. Sometimes things don't go the way I want them to go, and in the end, when there's nothing to be done, when I am really exhausted and feeling bad about things that didn't go the way I wanted them to, I pacify myself by repeating a line I read in *The Fault in our Stars* – "The world is not a wish-granting factory."

This gives me a bit of relief. Maybe the thought that everyone has to go through this phase gives me courage. Sometimes I wonder if I am a sadist, taking pleasure in other's trouble. Again, if we look at it from a different POV, those troubles help those people learn something new, so I take pleasure in watching them grow. Who cares? I recollect one such incident, where I didn't have a breakthrough in what I was trying to achieve -

The clock hands formed a 150° angle, depicting 7AM (or 7PM. But it was morning). I was desperately trying to come up with some story that I could proudly boast as 'Mine'. People were slowly waking up to the chirping of the birds. Some ignored the call of the birds and continued sleeping until someone came and shook them and then ta da! They woke up. I was sitting in the living room with my laptop. My achievements, the trophies, the medals, certificates, all were staring at me from behind the shelf sitting in front of me. I couldn't let them down. I was their master; they just shouldn't see me in such a weak state. I observed my surroundings, concentrated on the voices, the noises. Birds chirping, people screaming, tires screeching, fan rotating, horn honking, me breathing.

But none of these voices compelled me to write something. Not a story, not an essay, a poem. Nothing. So, I decided to distract myself. I imagined myself as the Prime Minister of India, giving a speech to the whole country via television –

"India! The land I live in. The land of cultures. The land of colours. The land of brotherhood. But also, the land of darkness and grief.

India has evolved as one of the world's hugest power. Over the years, politics and poverty have taken over our country. The economy of our country is moving in a K shape. The rich are getting richer, and the poor, poorer. There are many in our country who are not much different from the British. Wanting to suck everyone dry till nothing but they are left. Money and power is all that matters to them. They are in a hysteria, in greed of money and power. They don't give a damn as to what happens to us folk. And there are few, who really hope and work for and towards a better tomorrow, a better India. Let us be a part of those few people. Let us fulfil our karma towards our country.

Let us be a part of a better tomorrow."

And then, the camera switched off and I came back to reality. I liked the speech. Maybe I should have written it down.

Then I realized, you don't need a plot, characters, twist, climax and all that mumbo-jumbo to cook up a story. Not that they are useless. But you can do without them. You needn't be JK Rowling to write a story or publish a book. There'll be times when things will simply go kaput; worry about them, sure. But don't waste your time and energy feeling guilty or bad or depressed or sad. Just be true to yourself, and the story (or poem or essay or whatever) will come by itself, without any effort.

20

A Pome

When you write a pome,
 Be sure to open your dome,
 Let the thoughts flow in
Use one and put the rest in the bin.

When you write a stori,
 In your mouth place a berry,
 Chew and chew and write and write
 Until the moon says, "It's night!"

When you write an essae,
 Do not worry about the bessay,
 Be sure to call Caroll
 And have a flute of faroll.

When you drink some watter,
 I tell you, you won't get fatter
 Or you can mix
 Scotch and water as a quick fix.

When you eat some fud,
   Make sure it's not sud,
   If it's not very gud
   Then it would be very bud.

21

How Krishna Got His Name

Mathura, 3228 BCE

"Jai Ram Shri Ram Jai Jai Ram" Devaki kept chanting these words in her mind as thoughts rushed in and out of her mind faster than the wind. King Vasudev had been forced to abdicate his throne, and along with it, his kingdom, the Vrishnis. Kansa, his brother-in-law had taken the throne by deception, and thrown the former King and Queen of Vrishnis, Vasudev and Devaki, into the dungeons, accusing them of treason. Lines of worry were showing on Vasudev's head; his wife was pregnant. *Kansa has already killed seven of my sons. I will not let him kill my eighth offspring. I will save my eighth progeny. My eighth son will slay Kansa. I hope Guru Sandipani is right.*

"Vasudev, what will we name our child?", Devaki asked.

"It has to be something great. Something, "

"What about Abhyankara? The one, who does removes fear of evil from people's minds."

"No. I have decided what to name him. His name alone, must instill fear in people. He will slay Kansa."

"What? Is my eighth son going to slay Kansa? But what will we name him?"

"Maharishi Sandipani had told me this. He told me, that when Kaliyug begins, and evil assumes its worst form, then a saviour shall rise. The saviour will be our eighth son. Our progeny will slay Kansa."

"You didn't answer my question. What will we name him?" There was a hiatus after this. After what seemed like an eternal silence, Vasudev took a deep breath, then looked up, as if drawing energy from the skies. Energy to tell his wife the name of his son.

"Mukund"

22

Holiday

H up hup hup let's go to school,
    Brush your teeth and have milk cool
    Forgot your homework, forget your books?
The very same ones for which you fell into soups?
Wear your socks and then wear shoes,
Vice-versa will get you a bruise!
Keep your bottle handy,
And make sure your glasses are trendy!
Write down your notes and complete your homework,
In front of your class, you don't wanna look like a jerk!
Back to home, have a bath,
Then geometry, history and math!
Then sleep tight and have a nice dream,
'Cause when you wake up, you don't wanna scream –

"I don't wanna go to school,
Teachers and friends uncool
I don't wanna go there today,
When will I get a holiday?"

23

Home Sweet Home

I'm flying in the air,
   The ground is white
   I wear a heavy suit,
I feel very tight.

I long for home,
   Its warmth and comfort
   What wouldn't I give,
   To wear again a pant and a shirt?

I'm back in the ship,
   I open up my suit
   All sorts of gadgets and devices,
   The existence of which, I want to refute.

I long for home,
   The laughter and the mirth,
   Oh, what wouldn't I give
   To be back on Planet Earth?

24

Sayonara

Things come and go,
  Winds blow and waters flow,
    Opportunities and people quickly I didn't identify,
The only thing I can do now is say Goodbye.

25

Topsy-Turvy

The night when I lay on the grass,
   I was sure there was a fault in the stars,
   The stars were chirping,
And the crickets were blinking.

Meteors lifted from the sky,
   And whooshed to the ground,
   The sky was green,
   And the grass was black indeed.

The star-ants bit me,
   And the grass poured a drizzle
   The winds blew the stars,
   And meteors shook the grass.

This weird fiction,
   I tried to get out of,
   When nothing else worked,
   I woke up.

26

What I Feared when I was 10 and 15

Fear is the bug on your hand,
    Fear is your watch lost in the sand
    In skydiving it is the chute,
In your house it's the thief who loots
It's the vulture in the sky,
In business it's the customer who doesn't buy
In India it was the British,
Now it sounds childish
But in childhood it was a monster,
And on the beach it's a lobster.

27

Her Last Wish

Bask in the sunshine,
    Or dance in the air,
      What does a flower do,
  Who has three days to live?

She wants to fly in the sky,
  Be the apple of everyone's eye
  She wants to run in the fields,
  Alas, she has only three days to live.

See her progeny spring,
  See their buds bloom,
  But all that she can only presume,
  For she has three days till her doom.

She wishes to be decked
  up like a queen, with
  Mascara and lipstick on,
  Barring there'll never be another dawn.

28

Question

This saying comes down from times primeval,
No man is good, and no woman evil
It is only thoughts that get misunderstood,
No man is evil and no woman good.

You, along with your opponent
Are equally good and bad,
Neither you are right, nor is she wrong
There's no reason to sulk and be sad.

They created a confusion,
As to who's bad and good,
You'll know only when,
The societal storm you've withstood.

About the Author

Aaditya Gajra is a 15-year young avid reader from Hyderabad. He is a full-time student and half-time graphic designer. Very studious in nature, he is a perfectionist. Not to mention that he is quite lazy, he is filled to the brim with leadership qualities. The fact that he loves cooking cannot hide that he is also tech-savvy. He loves music beyond measure and is an aspiring actor. He is a born rebel, going against all society norms and rules. His parents see him as 'Highly Inflammable' (very short-tempered). He is quite emotionally sensitive. His grandmother often remarks that he is as straight as a Jalebi.

Though his description sounds eccentric, he's a very interesting person to interact with. He writes back when you drop an email at gajra.aaditya@gmail.com

You can connect with me on:
🔗 https://www.goodreads.com/author/show/21793917.Aaditya_Gajra